I0606647

Dedication

I, Donald C Robertson Sr, wholeheartedly dedicate this book to all my contributors whose ideas, laughter, love, and support have been the foundation of my journey as a storyteller, academic, and Author. Without your encouragement and belief in me, this colorful world of storytelling would never have come to life.

To my beloved family, my wife Willene Robertson, my children Danielle and Donald Robertson Jr. who has been my constant pillars of strength and inspiration.

You have shaped me into the person I am today and have been the driving force behind my creative endeavors. Your unwavering love and encouragement have lifted me through challenges and celebrated my triumphs. This book is a tribute to the love and warmth you have bestowed upon me every step of the way.

Acknowledgments

Writing this book has been a fulfilling and transformative journey, and I am deeply grateful to the many individuals who have played a significant role in making it possible. Their support, guidance, and encouragement have been invaluable, and I would like to extend my heartfelt acknowledgments to the following: My Family: To my family, the foundation of my strength and inspiration. Thank you for standing by me, understanding the demands of the creative process, and offering unwavering support. Your belief in me and your love have been my guiding lights throughout this endeavor.

The Readers: Lastly, I extend my deepest gratitude to all the readers who will embark on this literary adventure. Your curiosity and openness to explore new narratives make the world of literature a wondrous place. It is my sincerest hope that my stories touch your hearts and leave a positive impact on your lives.

With a heart full of gratitude and appreciation, I thank each and every one of you for being a part of this book's creation and for supporting me as an author.

Sincerely,

Donald Robertson Sr.

About the Author

Donald C. Robertson Sr. is a trailblazing Black American author born in St. Louis, Missouri, during the vibrant and transformative 1960s. With a penchant for writing children's books that address sensitive issues in a fun and comical style, Robertson's colorful presentations have captured the hearts of young readers and adults alike. Through his work, he shares his life adventures, struggles, and breakthroughs, exemplifying how he fearlessly confronts challenges with humor, courage, and acceptance. His captivating storytelling delves into his personal journey and the influential people in his life, including family and friends, who have shaped him into the person he is today, instilling vital values and a resolute positive attitude.

Early Life and Inspirations: Donald C. Robertson Sr. was born into a bustling and culturally rich environment in St. Louis, Missouri. Growing up during the Civil Rights Movement, Robertson experienced firsthand the impact of societal changes and racial discrimination. It is from these experiences that he drew inspiration for his later works, focusing on promoting inclusivity, diversity, and acceptance through his children's books.

Bug Bottoms Creek

There's this tiny village in a super remote valley in the deepest forest of Anapeia. The town is quite similar to yours in many ways. In that, the residents loved to enjoy enormous meals, dance, and sing, and when it came to fashion well Paris had nothing on these folks.

Come closer, you might have to stretch your eyeballs so you can see and enjoy the wonderful excitement going on here at Bug Bottom Creek. If you haven't guessed it by now, this is a village of insects, not just one species but species from all over the world, who have settled here to create a wonderful, safe environment for all bugs. Their core beliefs were friendship, diversity, family, acceptance, and partying!!!!!

As the bushes are moved back we are able to peek into an amazing world that most people often never see. You have to look very closely, because they purposely hide their village to keep out unwanted guest. There nestled behind a few tall trees and to large hills side by side you will find the entrance to Bug Bottoms Creek, the village of bugs families all living together as one community. A village of loud music, party going, dancing, singing bugs. That's right BUGS.

.Each of these bugs was very different in species, type, and appearance. Some were tall, some small, some crawled, and hopped, and some even had wings that allowed them to fly all over the forest. However, despite their difference, they got along very well and learned to celebrate and joke about what they noticed the most was their strange little Bottoms which came in multiple sizes, colors, and shapes, and they often conducted Bug Pageants and talent shows to celebrate their anatomical uniqueness, more specifically their Bottoms to select the most impressive bug Bottoms in the village.

Let's get to know some of the residents of Bug Bottom Creek and identify some of their unique characteristics. First let's meet Hank is the first mate to the Queen Shaquisha the mother of all the ants. They keep her busy taking care of all those baby ants. The ants have three main parts: head, thorax, and abdomen. They have large bulbous heads, small thorax, and large round bottoms, which made them the perfect target for jokes and funny nicknames, such as bumble buns and jelly beans.

All day long, they worked extremely hard, frequently spotted following one another in a line to and from their homes, while transporting food or construction materials for their ant hills. They were very strong and would often work together to carry objects 5 times their own size.

Next, we have John. the leader of the Beetles, not the singing group from London, although he considered himself a great signer. He often sang to his crews of workers as they gathered leaves and food from the forest grounds. He was a great organizer and well-liked and respected by all the other bugs. The beetles all had thick armored shells, making their bottoms incredibly rough. They called themselves rock Bottoms and onlookers frequently witnessed them rolling around on their backs, utilizing their strong legs and sturdy bottoms to regain an upright position.

Meet Charles, the leader of the butterflies, he had a narrow head and long skinny body with large beautiful wings. He was a handsome insect and the women would lose their minds when flew past them. His group also had the most beautiful multi-color wings and long narrow bottoms.

They used their Bottoms to steer and navigate throughout the forest, as they pollinated the flowers and plants.

Their Bottoms were known as gossamer glutes, and they used them according to the other bugs to flirt and flutter around the forest, leaving a rainbow trail behind them.

Next, there was Flo, the leader of the ladybugs. She and her crew had a small head, sharp claws, two elytra which are like wings, and tiny painted oval shells which covered their round bottoms. They were called Picoln Peaches; they were considered show stoppers because everywhere they went bugs would stop to see their beautiful, spotted shiny shells. Often they left little trails of glitter, a sure sign that they had just left the area.

Another interesting group was the Grasshoppers, and their leader was Janet. A tall, long slender body bug, with round narrow butt and large arms and huge strong longs. They hopped around and played leap frog as they moved through the grass.

Next, there is Bobo, the crickets' leader. He was full of joy and always happy as he jumped and hopped around the village. He would say good morning, and other nice things as he greeted the other bugs. The crickets all had large head, enormous bellies, skinny prickly legs, and round bouncy bottoms. They enjoyed hopping and making people happy with their soft cheerful music. They were known as fiddler sticks.

One of the village's favorites meets Scott the leader of the fireflies. He was one of the most popular bugs in the village because he led the village's entertainment committee and was in charge of all the shows and events. The fireflies had small heads, thin bodies, and a large twinkling bottom that glowed in the dark.

They used their bottoms to entertain the other bugs during events and light up the night like little lanterns on a hot, dark summer evening. These bugs were called Flicker Fannies and would often light up the night with their glow from their luminous gray Bottoms.

And you know that no story can be told without the hometown hero Sargent Zookie. His small head has eyes that protrude like binoculars on each side, clear color wings, and he is always covered in moss. Sargent Zookie was a Moss Beetle who was the village veteran of past wars, and had seen many years here at Bug Bottom Creek.

He was in charge of the Bug Bottom Creek army reserve and often reminded the bugs to always be prepared for intruders. He used the camouflage of the moss in the forest to hide his wings and bottoms, making himself almost invisible among the trees, and becoming a brilliant soldier.

Zookie often talked about the great encounters he had experienced and how pasted bug villages had he faced terrible battles. However, with his great gift skills, and quick thinking, they won the day by sneaking behind enemy lines and informing the bugs of the best way to destroy the enemy's plans. Sargent Zookie often warned the villagers of Bug Bottoms to stay alert because one of these days, our enemies will return and we better be ready. The older people respected him and prepared but the younger children just laughed and ignored him because they knew nothing of war, just singing and dancing.

Zookie often talked about the great encounters he had experienced and how pasted bug villages had he faced terrible battles. However, with his great gift skills, and quick thinking, they won the day by sneaking behind enemy lines and informing the bugs of the best way to destroy the enemy's plans. Sargent Zookie often warned the villagers of Bug Bottoms to stay alert because one of these days, our enemies will return and we better be ready. The older people respected him and prepared but the younger children just laughed and ignored him and continued to laugh and play. because they knew nothing of war in their short lifetime.

The Mayor of Bug Bottoms was Clyde. He was a Shield Bug with a small head, a small body, with a large cover over his bottoms. When disturbed or frightened, Clyde could change the color of his whole body and Bottoms to blend in with his environment. Going unnoticed and avoiding immediate danger.

He was no fighter and often look for ways to avoid conflicts. Which made him the perfect Politian for Bug Bottom Creek, as he often used to talk to the bug community and could really stir up a crowd. People liked and trusted him.

Last but not least, let us not forget the janitor of the forest Stinky the Dung Beetle. Stinky got his name from his profession, hauling trash, leaves, rotten fruit, and dung from all over the village and surrounding areas. His real name was Edward, but only one person took the time to know him or call him by his real name.

Edward did have one friend, Charles, the leader of the butterflies, who would stop by and talk with Edward at the end of each day. Charles asked about his day and made sure that Charles understood the importance of his job to the community. Edward appreciated that and thanked him for his friendship.

Edward loved people and took his job seriously, providing a clean environment for his friends in the village. He often went on with his business, with no one saying hello or ac-knowledging his presence. He had a small round head, pow-erful arms, muscular legs, and a small but. The bugs often saw Stinky moving large piles of sticks and dung that weighed many times his own. Edward had several brothers, who helped him remove waste from the village, and could often be seen tirelessly moving dung/waste from one end of the forest to the other by pushing it, rolling it, and carrying it to their stockpile on top of the two hills.

These bugs are just a few of the bugs in Bug Bottom Creek that made the community a special place to live. These bugs may have had bottoms of all different shapes, colors, and sizes. However, they celebrated their differences by joking around about their unique features, their usefulness, and who had the biggest, the most beautiful, and so on.

They knew everyone was special in their way, and that having a funny, quirky bottom was just part of being a bug. They were content with their happy lives in the village, and little did they know how important their differences would play in their survival.

So party on little bugs, shake those bottoms, and do the bug booty bump at the Club Oak Tree Stump until the next workday begins.

As days went on, everyone was going about the routine schedules in the tiny little village, the ants were busy foraging for food; the ladybugs were flying around catching aphids, and the crickets were playing their merry tunes.

But little did they know that there was danger looming and heading their way. At that very moment, a colony of carnivorous termites burst into the forest and embarked on a path that would lead them directly through the ladybugs and crickets' claimed territory, intending to establish it as their own.

The first to spot the termite army was a group of ants, they had never seen these bugs in the forest before, ran straight to Hank, their leader, and told him what they had seen. Hank and the ants went to town running and shouting to the other bugs in the village that they had seen some strange creatures coming towards the village.

The ant leader described the invaders to the Clyde Mayor and Sargent Zookie, and it didn't take long for the bugs to realize the severity of the situation. These invaders were termites. Only a few of the bugs knew what termites were, or how dangerous the situation could be. Sargent Zookie provided a description of these invaders and what could be expected of them. The termites had sharp teeth, and wings, and were stronger than most bugs. The termites would fight to the death and leave no bug left alive.

Charlie the mayor called for a town meeting with all the bugs to discuss the upcoming danger and determine what they all should do. Some bugs said to fly away, others said hop over them and get far away, or hide until they pass us by. Charlie insisted that they all be calm and think about their action responsively.

However, a loud voice from the crowd said, NO! We will stand our ground and fight them and we will win, said, Sargent Zookie, your grandparents have fought them before during the great war.

We have the power together to defeat this enemy like we did before and run them away forever. All the bugs joined in as Sargent Zookie explained that it was our differences that allowed us to beat them before and, working together as one community of all bugs, we can do it again.

Although terrified and skeptical, the bugs reluctantly decided that every bug working together with their unique sizes, bottoms, skills, and experience could work together to defeat these invaders. Other leaders spoke up to lead the charge, the fireflies, with their glowing bottoms, formed a team to scout and monitor the movement of the termites.

Teddy, the youngest of all the beetles, yelled out, we can beat them, they will think twice about coming back here again.

The Beetles with their dependable rock Bottoms strategically placed themselves around the perimeter right outside the village to stop the termites from getting any closer to the village

The battle began at the entrance of the village; the first bugs to attack the termites were the crickets with their powerful bouncy bottoms that would jump up and on the backs of the termites, destroying their formation and scattering their soldiers.

The fireflies shined their light in the eyes of the termites which made it hard for them to see the bugs surprise attacks.

The ladybugs, with their sharp claws and cute little Bottoms, bravely took on the termites in one-on-one aerial combat above the village.

The butterflies, with their gossamer glutes, fluttered about, keeping the morale of the bugs high. They flew over the entire battlefield cheering on the ladybugs and the crickets and striking fear in the termites as they would zoom down on the termites and buzz them as they went by.

The grasshoppers eagerly joined in the fight. They would emerge out of nowhere, jump over enemy lines, and surprise the invaders. They often could wipe out an entire group before they knew what hit them. Kicking the soldiers and stomping them with their large legs. The grasshoppers came prepared with their foot stopping shoes on just for the termites. After a good stomping from the grasshoppers, the termites would drop their weapons and run and hide.

In order to get the advantage it was clear that the bugs needed to know what the Termite leader and his army had plan for their next attack. So, Sargent Zookie and Clyde the mayor decided to invade the camp of the Termites and learn their plans. Sargent Zookie crouched low, his body perfectly blended into the surrounding moss. His mossy green shell helped him look like just another patch of forest floor as he crept closer to the towering walls of the termite camp.

The termites were up to something, and Sargent Zookie needed to know what. He scuttled from rock to rock, leaf to leaf, his big eyes peeking out from his moss disguise. The entrance to the camp was heavily guarded by soldier termites, their sharp mandibles clicking in unison. But Zookie had a plan.

Zookie and Clyde used their ability to camouflage themselves, sneaked into the camp, and got really close to the termite leader's tent. Zookie hid in a tree in the corner of the tent, and could hear everything the termite leader and the termite generals were saying. . Mayor Clyde showed real courage, as he could cloak himself and sat right on the termite leader's desk.

He waited until a breeze rustled the leaves, making everything in the forest move slightly. Using this moment of distraction, Mossy slipped past the guards and into the camp, sneaking toward the large termite mound where the secret meeting was happening.

WIPED OUT THE BUG VILLAGE
WIPED OUT THE BUG VILLAGE

The termite leader, Demo, had a ruthless reputation as a veteran of many wars and had never experienced defeat. When he invaded a village, he would tell his men to kill them all! No surrender and wipe out the entire village, leaving no one alive.

Demo gathered his men and discussed his plans to overtake the Bug Bottoms Village. First, he would have a group fly over the village and attach from the rear. They should make their way to the entrance, so the other troops can enter the village with the entire army. We will strike at dawn while they sleep, and they will never know what's coming until it is all over

Inside, the termite generals were gathered around a small pile of leaves, using twigs to draw out their secret attack plans against the bugs. Sargent Zookie strained his ears to catch every detail. "We'll attack at dawn," one termite said, "while the bugs are distracted by the morning dew."

Zookie smirked under his mossy covering. He had the information he needed. Now all he had to do was sneak back out without being noticed.

Clyde the shield bug had also heard the termite plans and could not wait to get back to the camp so they could develop a counter attack against the taramite army.

Zookie and Clyde waited till Demo retired for the evening and made their way back to their Bug Bottoms headquarters for the valuable information they had collected. Zookie then devised a plan to counteract the attempted surprise attack by the termites.

Zookie together with Clyde developed their plan then issued instructions to the other bugs to catch the termites by surprise. He assigned the ladybugs, the butterflies, and the fireflies to intercept the flying termites as they attempted to attack the rear. The beetles would continue to hold the line in front of the entrance with the grasshoppers, and everyone else would make lots of loud noise.

The fireflies shined their bright lights on the termite army to blind them from seeing a clear view of the Bug Bottom entrance to the town or the actual numbers of bugs waiting to attack.

The crickets play their music as a distraction, making the termites believe they were all at the front entrance of the village and that the rear was unmonitored. Hopefully, this would keep the termites from advancing through the front entrance until they could use their secret weapon.

At dawn, it all began as planned, with the termites sending their flying squadron to advance from the rear. Charlie, Scot, and Flo ordered their army to start their surprise attack, catching the termites totally off guard and wiping out the entire group, spraying them with honey, causing their wings to stick together, and then crashing to the ground. Upon hearing that his termites had been defeated, Demo decided to assemble the entire army at the village entrance

51

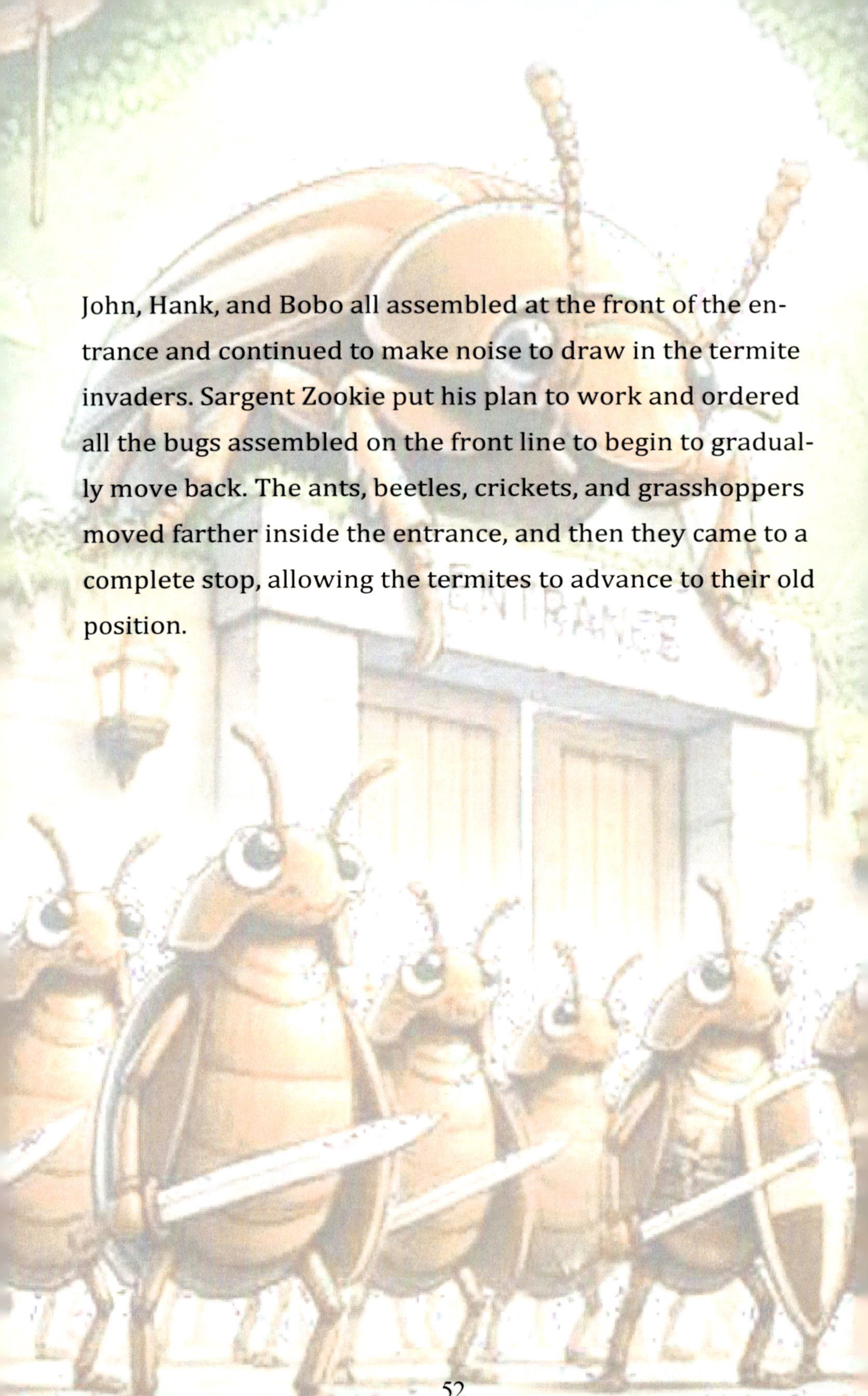

John, Hank, and Bobo all assembled at the front of the entrance and continued to make noise to draw in the termite invaders. Sargent Zookie put his plan to work and ordered all the bugs assembled on the front line to begin to gradually move back. The ants, beetles, crickets, and grasshoppers moved farther inside the entrance, and then they came to a complete stop, allowing the termites to advance to their old position.

♪♫F!

Sargent Zookie ordered his army to gradually move back once again farther into the entrance of the village, then stop and hold the line. The termite army advanced once again and waited to see what would happen next. Finally, Zookie ordered his army to retreat into the village walls screaming and yelling, as if they were giving up as they proceeded through the entrance of the village.

Demo said, we have finally broken their spirit to fight and now they are running like cowards. Yes, run said Demo. Now you will see my mighty army, yes, run in fear. Demo order assemble all our troops at the entrance and prepare to attack.

Zookie said to the bug army, now we have them just where we want them, and it's up to our secret weapon to finish the job. Zookie , Clyde, Hank, Janet, and all the other bugs told the other bugs to yell at the top of their little voices. Now!

Stinky let them have it!

Stinky and his siblings sitting high above the entrance dropped the boulders, sticks, and yes dung, collected from all the animals in the village forest over many years of cleaning the village, onto the termite army. You see this is where Stinky and his siblings stored the dung and boulders, and sticks collected for many years.

Stinky dropped these items on the termites. POW take that! The termites were crushed by the boulders, and sticks, and the others were all covered in dung, and they were so humiliated they dropped their weapons and retreated.

After covering the entire army, the bugs from Bug Bottoms continued to pummel the termites. The Ants attached with their bumble buns, the Beetles with their armored Bottoms, Grasshoppers jumped and pounced on the backs of the termites, and the crickets stomped them with their strong legs and bouncing Bottoms, the butterflies and the fireflies buzzed over the heads of the retreating termites, as they ran off in fear. Each bug used its unique bottoms, skills, and abilities to attack the small group of remaining termites.

COMP!

Sargent Zookie found the termite leader in a mound of dung and trash, with minor injuries to his head, teeth shattered, and a broken leg. He asked Demo, well do you surrender? Are do you want me to unleash the rest of my army? Demo said no that he surrendered and would leave and never return to this stinky village ever again. Zookie cut off Demo's wings as a sign of final defeat and sent him packing with his defeated, scattered army.

Speaking of Stinky, well, what about that Stinky and his siblings? The bug that everyone in the village ignored and laughed at because of the service he provided for the village. Charles, his one loyal friend, stood up and began cheering for Edward, his name is Edward and he saved the entire village. Teddy still riding on Edwards back shouted three cheers for Edward. They all chanted Edward! Edward! Thank you.

He and his family were never laughed at again, in fact they were considered heroes and treated with honor and respect.

Victory had been achieved, and the bug's families threw a fantastic party with Edward as their special guest. They presented him with a water collector to catch the rain and store it so he and his brothers could shower at the end of each day. Then they began to party!

The Bugs from Bug Bottom bumped their buns, and bounced their bottoms, and the crickets played a happy song with their musical legs. They had come together as a village, team, and family and fought to defend their homes. They learned to respect everyone and to understand that everyone plays a role in a community, no matter how small to make a village strong. What had seemed to make them different brought them all together. They laughed and joked about how they had come together and how their unique bottoms had made all the difference.

The crickets played their fiddles and made the bugs all dance and sing.

All the bugs started to dance and celebrate and give thanks for their victory. They thanked Edward and his siblings for their efforts.

Victory had been achieved, and the bug's families threw a fantastic party with Edward as their special guest. They presented Edward and his siblings with a water collector to catch the rain and store it so he, and his brothers could shower at the end of each day. Edward and his family were so pleased and could not wait to use the new showers. Then they began to party!

Edward and his brother could not wait till the end of the day to bathe in the fresh water to remove the dirt and smell from hauling dung and trash all day.

The dung beetles and their families were very grateful of the leaf waterfall, were they enjoyed the fresh water that ran off of the leaves.

Many of the other Dung Beetles began to build their own leaf showers for their families and other bugs to share.

Overcoming the danger and rallying together as one, the bugs were able to use their unique sizes, colors, skills, and bottoms to defeat their enemies. They also realized the importance of valuing every bug no matter how what. You never know who you might have to rely on when trouble comes to your village. Always appreciate your similarities and look for opportunities to celebrate your differences mayor Clyde told the bugs. Diversity, Equity, and Inclusion is what won the day for the little bugs of Bug Bottom Creek.

With that in mind the bugs went back to what they did bests Parting, Singing, and Dancing. At the end of each party the bugs would select one bug to make the winner of the Bug Bottom Party.

They would all line up and strut their stuff across the stage,
trying to impress the judges.

Those with wings would fly, some would crawl, and others
would hop across the stage.

All of the bugs stop and listen to see who the winner will be this time around. I think the judges are about ready to announce the winner, says the Mayor.

Congratulations Ms. Firefly, and to all the bugs of Bug Bottom Creek. They are all winners today and will celebrate and return to their wonderful live.

The End

Copyright 2024 by DCR BOOKS INC. All rights reserved.

Made in in to the USA

Maryland Heights, MO

09/19/2024

www.ingramcontent.com/pod-product-compliance
Lightning Source LLC
Chambersburg PA
CBRC090956100726
47911CB00007B/172